Publisher's Note: This is a work of fiction. Names, characters, places, and
incidents are a product of the author's imagination. Locales and public
names are sometimes used for atmospheric purposes. Any resemblance to
actual people, living or dead, or to businesses, companies, events,
institutions, or locales is coincidental.

Edited by Aquila Editing

Cover Designer: Cameron Hart from Grown With Hart

HELLO FROM ABBY!

Thanks for picking up my book! If you want to check out more of my titles, or to subscribe fo reader alerts, please visit my author page at www.authorabbyknox.com.

Happy reading!

RECKLESS IN RUINS

RECKLESS ROYALS; A COMPANION SHORT STORY

ABBY KNOX

RECKLESS IN RUINS

For readers familiar with the Reckless Royals series, this is a short story about Uther, the head of palace security, and Sable, the palace stylist.

Uther

Protecting the queen is my only job, and I'm the best at it. Lately, though, one woman has destroyed my indestructible focus. *Sable.* Even her name renders me unable to think of anything but how soft she might feel against me. The palace stylist insists on pestering me about measurements and uniforms, but the more I dismiss her, the bolder she becomes. When she finally takes things a step too far, she threatens to push me right over the edge.

About the series:

Reckless Royals is a tropey, soapy, swoony and sexy collection of happily-ever-after romances. It's got everything: Bad boys, grumpy, gorgeous heroes, strong, sassy heroines, arranged marriages, divorce pacts, marriage pacts, and lots of surprises along the way.

It's all packed into one royal family with five stand-alone love stories to tell! No cheating, no cliffhangers. Five separate HEAs with epilogues.

Reading order

Favored Prince -- semi-secret identity, prince hero, American heroine, virgin hero

Bad Prince -- misunderstood bad boy/playboy, uptight heroine, arranged/coerced marriage, forced proximity, two people/one bed.

Wild Prince -- prince hero, waitress heroine, two people/one bed, the outdoorsy grumpy one loves the indoorsy sunshine one.

Forgotten Prince -- Marriage pact, surprise identity, long lost childhood friends, quirky small town.

Stolen Crown -- Forbidden romance, brother's best friend, princess heroine/gamekeeper hero.

1

ther

My top security officer has bad news for me.

Apprehension clouds Edgar's face as he exits the Bentley, carrying a letter from the palace. I zero in on the queen's tell-tale stationery. The officer's stride battles against the stiff sea wind sweeping over the grassy cliff, giving me time to remove any trace of shock from my face. My men never see me appearing shocked. Or worried, or any other emotion.

I am the unflappable Captain Uther Nancarrow. The silent minder. Head of palace security, and the tireless bagman for the queen.

The public sees me as nothing but solely focused on the royal family of Gravenland, and that letter changes nothing.

Not until I open it.

I move into the shadow of the ancient stones to stave off the battering wind. Edgar hands me the letter. This is it. I'm fired. My years of unquestioning service to the protection and service of Queen Hilde are about to come to an end.

Strange that the queen would choose now and not the end of my shift. Have I been so derelict in my duties she needs to replace me immediately? In the middle of a security sweep ahead of a royal engagement?

"From the palace, sir."

I rarely feel the urge to engage with sarcasm with one of my men. I resist that urge now, and simply thank Edgar before opening the letter.

Edgar stands there expectantly for a moment, as if I might share the contents of this missive with him.

"You're dismissed."

"Y-yes, Captain," he says, his voice cracking. He leaves for the Bentley at the speed of someone being shot from a cannon, eager to avoid a dressing down.

At first glance, the queen's handwriting seems shaky.

"Dear Uther,

It has come to my attention that you've missed three fittings with the palace stylist. Please make arrangements to meet with Sable today without delay."

I squint at the lettering. An ordinary citizen would immediately recognize the queen's sweeping S. The slash with which she crosses her T's. But I am not an ordinary citizen. This is forgery. This letter did not come from Queen Hilde.

I know exactly which persistent person wrote this. Only

one employee at the palace would dare try to get my attention this way, fearless of being put in handcuffs.

That insufferable woman.

Inexplicably, Sable is unintimidated by me. She addresses me so haughtily with her red lips, while her judging eyes rake over my frame as if amused by my large, ape-like stature. No doubt she's thinking about dressing me up in something fashion-forward, as she does with the royal siblings. Well, I'm not one of her paper dolls. My traditional kilt and suit jacket are perfectly suitable to carry out my duties, as it has been for the security detail of generations before me.

The palace stylist can't seem to take the hint that I don't need a change in uniform, not for me or for my men. Especially not from a woman with mocking eyes and a wry smile who can't wait to get her hands on me, a peasant who rose through the ranks on his own steam and grit.

Sable is so determined, she's deluded herself into thinking she can get away with imitating the queen? All in the name of fitting me in some dandy new color scheme to make the queen's Secret Service stand out. What that tiny, flamboyant woman doesn't seem to realize is the entire point of security is to blend in. We are bodyguards. Not backup dancers.

Sweat forms on my brow just thinking about all this harassment.

Still holding this ridiculous letter, I use the back of my hand to swipe at my forehead.

Hell, the paper even smells like Sable—that scent she designed herself in some exclusive laboratory in Paris, or so I've gathered. The scent is an odd choice for a woman like her, conjuring images of rose petals and fresh bed linens. With her long lashes, pouty lips, and pushy attitude, I would have thought her perfume would be spicier. Earthier.

What the hell is wrong with you, Uther? Thinking about perfume now? Get your head in the game.

With a snarl of frustration, I crush the letter in my hands. I stuff it into the leather sporran on my uniform kilt, stuffing it down along with my feelings about the letter's author.

I stalk toward the perimeter of Skelside Ruins, scanning the coastline for any signs of danger, any signs of possible threat to Her Majesty the Queen.

How dare I let one tiny, annoying, beautiful woman wreck my concentration? How dare I allow anyone to interfere with my job?

Walking the field helps me regain my focus. I'm grateful for the battering wind sweeping over the cliffs, knocking the nonsense and silliness out of me.

Skelside Ruins is a two-thousand-year-old fortress that pre-dates the influence of mainland Europe on this tiny island country. It is one of a few ancient sites in Gravenland that bears no mark from the centuries of rule from England, France, Germany, the Netherlands. Today, it's little more than a maze of stone staircases, a few damaged walls, a turret, and a sprawling stone foundation. As I sweep the grounds, I begin to feel restored. The connection to my ancestors girds me up. I am proud to serve a monarchy that aims to preserve this site for future generations.

It doesn't look like much, but Skelside Ruins was once one of many imposing structures that marked the territory of ancient tribes. Millennia of chieftains and warriors fought bloody battles on this hill, long before the Vikings and the Normans invaded.

Ensuring everything is ready for the queen's appearance here this morning doesn't take me long. The media area is cordoned off, keeping nosy reporters from damaging the precious remaining structures. I have two men at that location. A few members of the general public—mostly those whose work is related to historic preservation—have been invited to attend the ceremony. I have one man at that station for crowd control. The queen will soon arrive and I'll escort her personally to the podium on the site that is thought to be the site of a former great hall. Or an inner courtyard; the debate amongst archeologists continues.

Luckily that's not my job to know. I just have to ensure safety.

When I'm sure all is ready for the public's arrival, I take a moment to appreciate the view of the North Sea from the top of the turret.

The weather has taken its toll on this structure, and it seems that keeping random people away is the least of the queen's worries.

In fact, it's questionable whether I should even be up here myself, as the stone ledge of the round turret is hardly safe for the average tourist. I'm about to finish my security sweep before anyone spots me up here, when I hear footsteps on the winding staircase below.

Shit! I'm caught.

Instinctively I turn to the noise. No one is supposed to arrive for another ten minutes.

My hand goes to my sidearm and I barrel down the steps, intent on scaring the shit out of whoever this might be. A reporter? A wayward citizen? Yet another tourist bent on stealing something from a sacred site? I'm not having any of it.

I fly around the corner and smack head on into a short, black-caped woman, who lets out a shriek of surprise. She loses her footing on the mossy steps, and, on instinct, I lunge.

Pinning her to the stone wall, my shouting echoes in this dank space. "This is a restricted area. You are detained by the order of Her Majesty the Queen. What is your name?"

The black-caped woman lifts her head, and the weak sunlight bleeding in through the gap in the stones catches on long, dark lashes and red lips.

The same red lips that haunt my dreams every damn night.

2

S able

I try to be silent as I follow Uther up the winding staircase.

Silence is a tall order, especially when the man I'm stalking—er, following—flashes muscled thighs as he marches up ahead of me.

The curse of a traditional black kilt. The strong legs are out there on display every day, his movements giving the barest hint at the soft hairs on his thick legs.

Every sighting of Uther's knees turns my insides to jelly.

Captain Uther Nancarrow is perfect in every way. And what do I do with perfection? I must create. I *need* to dress him. I swear, I'm not trying to be creepy, but tailor's measuring tape does give a girl an excuse to get good and close.

And now I'm face to face with the queen's chief security officer, who pins me against the damp, ancient stones.

Oh dear. I didn't think this through. I didn't think any of this through.

I can hardly breathe. And not because Uther's forearm, from elbow to wrist, presses against the length of my collarbone. The air catches in my throat in reaction to how absolutely lethal this man is up close.

I've admired him from a distance for so long.

Ever since I was promoted to the job as official stylist for the palace, I've been utterly fascinated by the tall, dark, silent man and the way he attends to the queen's every need with care and unwavering devotion. It's like watching someone sweetly hover around a beloved grandmother. He fascinates me because, for one thing, not even the queen's own children fuss over their mother this way. Likewise, Queen Hilde's attitude towards her children resembles that of a captain steering a ship full of undisciplined sailors who need constant reminders of duties and decorum.

But with Uther, she's different.

I don't know what it is about him, but watching him with her does something to me. The way he fetches her handbag, walks next to her, pulls out chairs, holds doors, and keeps the citizens from taking too much out of her. It makes me wish I was the queen for one day, if only to feel that blanket of protection around me.

What is that like?

"Sable," he grinds out. "What are you doing here?"

"I'm..."

My stronger self urges me to gather my senses: *Speak, Sable. You know exactly why you came here. You're not intimidated by anyone.*

"I'm just trying to get your measurements. I-I knew you'd be here."

Uther's nostrils flair. My nipples tighten.

"This is a restricted site."

"So you've said," I say softly.

"I'm supposed to be sweeping the area for security breaches."

"I know that, too. And, in turn, why won't you let me do my job? What I need requires so little of your time." It feels good to challenge him. I'm slightly braver than I was a second ago.

Uther's eyes widen as if he can't believe what he's hearing. "Why don't *I* let *you* do *your* job? Madame. You cannot be serious. You have done nothing but interfere with my duties for weeks. You send email after email to my office. You make appointments without checking with my staff…"

I huff, pushing against his hold on me that might as well be a steel girder. "Because you don't respond to my questions, so I had to be more proactive."

"You follow me around the palace, follow me to all the queen's appointments, staring at me, watching me, trying to break me down…"

"Break you down?" Now I'm confused.

"I've seen the way you look at me. I know what you think of me and my shabby, old-fashioned uniform. I know I didn't grow up with money and connections to the palace. I know when I open my mouth, I sound exactly like I came from. I'm a simple man with simple needs, and I don't need to fit in with the aristocracy, if it's all the same to you."

I let out the breath I'm holding as I process all of this.

"Sir. The conclusions you jump to are truly breathtaking. I don't care where you're from."

"Your snobbery says otherwise."

"My…snobbery?"

"I've seen the way you look down your nose at me."

I can't control the bewildered laugh that escapes me.

"That's a mean feat, considering I'm barely eye level with your chest."

"You know what I meant."

"I really do not, Captain."

"You taunt me. You pester me. You spend every waking hour attempting to get a rise out of me, up to the point of stalking me at a sacred site and forging a letter from the queen!"

Oh. That.

Maybe this is wrong of me, but I feel oddly satisfied that I've rankled this man so thoroughly. Well, I learned how to act out for attention the honest way: from childhood trauma.

"The queen sent that letter yesterday. That's why I'm here today, to finish the job, so I can get started on the new guard uniforms."

"Quit. Lying."

The standoff feels like an eternity, though it lasts scarcely more than a few seconds. "Fine! It was me who sent the letter."

"Do you have any idea the consequences for impersonating a monarch?"

"Actually, I don't. Because in no way is it possible that a law exists about something so preposterous."

Am I mistaken, or does a smile pull at his lip?

"I can have you in front of a judge by lunchtime," Uther seethes.

I circle my fingers around the girth of his tensed forearm and tug feebly. "You can let me go. I'm not a physical threat, you know."

"You are a threat in every way possible."

The wrinkles around his deadly cobalt eyes would be devastating if only I could get him to really smile at me.

Those hands could have their way with me, ruining me for anyone else. His hard, flat mouth could destroy me seven different ways. And he sees *me* as a threat?

"You say that I taunt you. Pester you. That I spent my waking hours trying to think of ways to provoke you. It's quite the opposite, sir. You spend an inordinate amount of time and energy avoiding me. It's *you* doing that. I'm simply carrying out palace duties, the same as you. And if I'm not wrong..." I pause to study the gentle bags under his fierce gaze. "...I'd say you're lying awake at night obsessed by how much I annoy you."

3

U ther

Slowly, I release the arm that pins her to the wall.

But I am no less outraged at her behavior.

"Are you finished?" I ask.

"For now."

"Let me show you something."

Not waiting for an answer, I turn and climb the stairs to the top of the turret, circled by a waist-high, crumbling ledge.

Sable follows me, and I study her face as she scans the sea in the distance, then turns toward the mountains, the forest, and the capital city's distant skyline.

"It's breathtaking up here," she comments.

Forgetting myself as the diffused sunlight hits her pink cheeks, I lean against one of the precariously loose stones. It tumbles and falls, crashing down to the mossy courtyard below. Sable gasps and runs to the edge, watching in horror. She turns to me in shock. "Why did you do that?"

It was an accident, but I stupidly play it off for reasons I myself don't understand. "That," I say, pointing to the empty square in the ledge, "is as easy as it is to take a shot at the queen if I'm not paying laser-focused attention."

"Destroying historic property is hardly the visual demonstration you think it is," Sable says, squaring her shoulders though she's showing signs of fear. Maybe now she'll leave me alone.

I close in on her.

"Do you want the queen to die? Is that what you want?" I grit out.

She steps backward, shaken. Her chin trembles. "No. My gods, what an awful scenario to think of."

Her voice breaks, a sound that claws at my chest.

"Well I do think of it. I think about every awful possible scenario, every second of every day. That's my job. Except now, these last weeks, I've been distracted. And do you know why?"

"No," she answers.

"Because I think only of you. You and your messages. Your emails. Your handwriting. Your perfume. You have driven me to distraction, and one day, it will cost us both. It could cost everyone in Gravenland everything we stand for."

Sable's throat bobs, and the gray morning light shines in her wet eyes. Her lips part, but no sound comes out. She looks cold, and I resist the urge to remove my coat to offer it to her.

"I-I'm so sorry, Captain," she says, barely a whisper. She blinks rapidly as I step toward her, fright in her eyes as tears rain down her delicate cheeks.

Bloody hell.

Before I realize what the devil I'm getting myself into, I've cupped her face and swiped away those damn tears. "Stop your crying now, little poppy." My words fall out in a heated whisper, my jaw tight.

I take Sable's mouth roughly with mine, absorbing her surprised gasp. My brain catches up with my body and confirms: yes, I'm kissing this woman. Yes, it's wrong. Yes, I should send her packing and finish this security sweep. But damn, her lips on mine is the most electrified moment in years. Maybe ever.

Sable's lips are warm and soft as I sweep my mouth and tongue over them. Her tears wet my cheeks, and her gasping breath morphs into tiny moans against my mouth. Her small sounds of surprise turn me inside out with need. For weeks, I've been trying so hard to put her out of my mind. I've been denying the fact that one good, thorough kiss is what it will take to get this woman out of my system.

Sable's curves feel dangerously good in my arms as she surrenders to the kiss. Her body relaxes. Her lips part. I let go of her face, determined to end this kiss here and now, but I find my arms instead reaching out for her, pulling her frame against my chest. Her arms circle my shoulders, and I'm falling into a soft haze of pure temptation. I let my tongue slip inside her mouth, meeting hers. Her tongue. Gods, Sable's mouth is wickedly addicting. My mind reels with her heavenly scent while, at the same time, the taste of her mouth and the soft breasts pushed against me threaten to drag me to hell. She tastes like fine champagne, stirring darker thoughts of spreading her open and drinking up every drop of her.

I lick hungrily into her mouth, provoking a moan from

her throat that makes my dick jump, straining against the heavy wool of my kilt.

Nothing about this is getting her out of my system. What an absolute fool I am.

Every lick, every touch, every breath, every brush of her lashes against my cheek only stokes the flames of need higher.

Her moans pull me closer and closer to the edge. I fully claim her mouth, gripping her close, squeezing her in places where I shouldn't be squeezing. Imagining things I shouldn't be imagining.

The queen's motorcade is waiting at the palace for my signal. But I'm keeping them all waiting because I have to have this. I have to have her.

Sable.

I imagined earlier that I was about to be fired, and now I'm manifesting that for myself.

Our bodies are so close I don't know if it's my heart pounding or hers that I feel.

My hands roam down her back, seizing her fleshy hips, squeezing her there.

If I leave now, I might still retain my job. I can blame what is sure to be my swollen, red mouth on an allergic reaction to something.

It takes all the strength inside me to pull away from Sable's kiss, and my body rages at the loss of contact.

"Uther? What's wrong?" Sable blinks up at me, hurt written all over her face. It's the pretend hurt of a spoiled child who's never been told no in her life. She knows exactly what's wrong. Everyone calls me Captain, yet she feels free to call me by my first name when she wants to. It's utterly unprofessional.

"Dammit, Sable," I seethe.

"I've done nothing wrong, so don't start something you can't finish."

My rumble of low laughter gets a come hither look from her. She runs her palm over my stomach, daring to explore inside my uniform jacket.

"You know what you've done to me," I rasp.

She smiles that familiar, haughty smile. "What have I done, exactly?"

I lean in, our mouths a whisper apart. "You want specifics?"

Sable nods, then laughs. "Please, no more visual aids involving old stones."

Covering her hand with mine, I guide her down to the front of my kilt.

Her eyes go wide with wonder. Sable's swollen lips part.

"This, Madame, is what you've done to me. And you'll be taking it raw."

4

Sable

The shiver that runs down my spine is unreal.

"Gods, yes. Please." I sound like a frightened kitten but my body screams for it.

Uther, the most mysterious and eligible bachelor among the palace's staff, has an erection that could split rock in half. It's big. It's long. And it's all because of me.

"Do you see? You see how difficult you are?"

"On the contrary," I say, gazing up at him with confidence, even as my cheeks blaze with heat. "I'm quite easy if you just do things my way."

I don't know if it's a growl, but some type of animal noise escapes him the moment before Uther's tongue goes to my mouth.

I whine as he wrenches my hand free of his cock, and

the next thing I know, I'm pressed against the stones, his erection nudging into my side.

My body cries out for more. If he won't let me keep touching him then I need him to touch me. My tight nipples ache. I take his hand and guide it under my cape, beneath the hem of my sweater. He knows what I want, and he forges onward, dragging that hand up, over my skin until he's cupping my breast. He groans into my mouth. "Sable."

He sounds so angry at himself, and yet everything he does is wonderful. That large hand cages around my breast, squeezing through the material of my bra. His movements tighten my aching nipple even more.

"You shouldn't be doing this," he grinds out, his mouth blazing a hot trail down my jawline and descending down my throat. "We...shouldn't..."

"We absolutely should."

His reply is nothing but a grunt of surrender. Not bothering to unhook my bra, Uther hurriedly wrenches the band down, and dips his head low. For the briefest of moments, the icy sea wind tweaks my suddenly bare nipples as his free hand lifts my sweater. The cold is then replaced by the protection of Uther's hot mouth. He's not a tentative lover by any means. Once he decides to taste my bare breast, he is all over me, switching from one to the other like a wild thing. He takes me into his mouth with long pulls, his tongue sweeping over my flesh, teasing me out until those buds grow so hard, making every inch of my skin feel so connected, I wonder if I might spontaneously come.

And then, my blood turns to lava as I feel Uther reach between my legs. I startle as his strong hand rucks up my skirt and finds its way to my thong. He snaps it against my flesh.

"Uther!"

"This is a one-time thing. That's it," he says.

My eyelids flutter closed at the sensation of his rough fingers exploring my pussy.

"Is it?"

"I said what I said, Madame," he insists even as his fingers glide between my folds.

"Yes, Captain."

My eyes still closed, I feel his mouth on my throat. His breath sends chill bumps over my skin as he speaks. "You're so damn wet for me, aren't you, my flower?"

My voice breaks. "Oh..." I am lost for words. My only awareness is in the way he strokes inside me, sliding one thick digit into my slick cunt. He called me his flower as if I were a delicate thing. Yet he provokes thoughts of how protective he is of the queen. I wish it were me he accompanied on walks. I wish it were me who this man guarded against the energy vampires of this world.

Uther's ragged breath heats my ear as he whispers. "I have one question."

"Wh...what's that?"

"Do you taste as good as you smell?"

"Do I...do I what?"

I'm far too focused on how turned on I am to comprehend what he's talking about.

To my body's dismay, Uther slowly removes his worshiping fingers from inside my skirt. My eyes fly open and I want to protest. The lack of contact nearly destroys me, and I shiver like a woman whose internal thermostat has inexplicably plunged to freezing. But then, I forget all about the frustrating fact that he's not diddling me anymore. I watch in fascinated shock as Uther slowly lifts his two moistened fingers to his parted lips, and noisily sucks them clean.

With our gazes locked, it feels as if he dares me to look away.

My gods, how I soak myself. How I wish his mouth were on me, forcing me to ride his face.

"And?" I ask.

Without warning, that hand is clamped around my throat. Not hard. Not squeezing. Holding me in place. Reminding me that I came to him and what he plans to do with me is punishment, in a way.

His voice is lethal as he presses his mouth to my ear. "Your honey is like no other. It could drive me mad."

My body screams for him but my voice is a squeak. "Take all of it you want."

Humor glints in his eye. "Is it all for me, then?"

"All for you," I say on a gasp. Embarrassed that I sound desperate, I wait for him to quickly end this. Decide that this was a bad idea and send me packing so he can get back to his very important work. I want him too much, and now he knows.

But Uther doesn't end this moment.

He goes deeper.

On a curse, Uther lowers himself onto his knees. I gasp at the sensation of his hands reaching up under my skirt and squeezing my thighs, massaging them for a brief moment.

"You'll feel like you're falling, little poppy. But I won't let you."

"I...what?"

Uther replies not with words. His head disappears under my knee-length skirt, and in the next moment, one of my legs is being hoisted over one beefy shoulder.

"Oh," I breathe.

And that's about all I'm able to say for the next several minutes as the queen's top guard flays me open with his mouth.

5

ther

This impossible woman fills me in every possible way.

Sable's plump cheeks overflow as I hold her body against me.

Her hot stickiness pours into my greedy mouth.

Her moans fill my head with longing to make her scream.

Sable trembles as I trace my tongue along the seam of her sex.

"Oh," she gasps when I spread her lips open and inhale her scent.

This woman who seems to spend every minute of every day talking endlessly with everyone around her, who greets every moment with words, words, and more words, is finally speechless.

I push my tongue inside and taste her sweet juice as Sable pushes forward, riding my face, demanding more.

I hear her fingers scrambling for purchase on the ledge, on the fabric of her skirt.

She finally rucks up the skirt and threads her fingers through my hair, making a mess of me.

But I can't care about that now. How can I think about my appearance when this goddess's plump little leg is hooked tight over my shoulder?

Her cries of pleasure clue me in to what she likes, and where, and I savor her as if I have all the time in the world. I cover her clit with my mouth and suck, even as I push one thumb inside her slick channel.

"Yes...oh...yes!"

"That's it. Come for me like a good little girl. Do as you're fucking told for once."

Sable body seizes around me. A strange, animal wheeze is ripped from her throat as she comes. "Fuck me...Uther!"

Her body shudders so sweetly, all I can think of is taking her to my bed and making that happen again.

"Oh, I intend to, little poppy. I'm going to fuck you right now. That's what you came here for, isn't it?"

She stares up at me in wonder as I rise up to kiss her face, her cheeks flushed from her orgasm.

"Admit it," I tell her.

"Is this an interrogation, Captain?" Sable asks weakly with a smile.

"This isn't a time for games."

"Yes! I admit it! I followed you here because I wanted you! Is that what you want to hear?"

It is. And I need to be inside her now.

Without another word, I kiss her deeply, sharing her taste with her.

And then I give the order.

"Turn around. And bend over the ledge."

Sable follows orders so well it hurts. I want to be fully facing her. I want her naked underneath me; I want to feel her bare breasts, taste and tease her nipples, and make her beg for more. I want to lose myself in her. But we don't have that kind of time.

My utility belt falls to the ground at my feet with a loud clank. Removing it gave a modicum of relief, but not enough.

"Spread your legs, little poppy."

Dropping her cape to her feet, she obeys. I drag my fingers up her thighs, slotting my hand in her crack.

Her body jerks at the touch.

My heart racing, I hike up my kilt and free my cock, pressing it against the split of her ass.

Sable's small, sexy moans threaten to undo me; the precum is already so far in the danger zone it's close to becoming an earnest release.

I press the tip between her lips and she automatically pushes back. "Why do you call me 'little poppy'?" Sable asks.

Before I answer, I lube myself in her wetness, the friction intensifying her aftershocks and going straight to my ego. I already know this will not get her out of my system. If anything, I'm addicted.

It's not until I thrust inside and she cries out that I give her an answer.

She's so tight...Sable is so tight and perfect...I nearly forget the question. Hell, I can barely recall my own name. And then, her fit around me changes me. Invigorates me.

"Because you are small yet the brightest thing in any

room," I murmur into the flushed shell of her ear as I pull out and slam back in again.

I continue, "Because your lipstick is redder than blood." I continue in this manner, reveling in the deep, thorough thrusts into her tight, welcoming hole. "You're simple...but demanding... intoxicating...unmistakable...fiery...and absolutely...totally...fucking...infuriating..."

Sable squeezes down so hard I might explode, and it takes everything in me to stay in the moment and not let go.

6

S able

This man, Captain Uther, is often referred to by royal watchers as "the silent minder."

The thought is laughable now.

This man? Silent? No way. He's got plenty to say while he's eight inches deep.

Uther's hearty thrusts punctuate each phrase.

"Totally...fucking...infuriating."

"I am not infuriating. You are!" My voice is a ragged squeak. I hear how childish that sounds even as the words leave my mouth. How else can I express myself when I can barely catch my breath while Uther's dicking the brain cells out of me?

He rocks into me with the rhythm of a runaway train, filling me, stretching me, and obliterating me.

The low rumble of laughter vibrates against my back, even through the layers of material between us. I have the overwhelming need to push him away and tear both our clothes off. I need to feel all that power against me.

But that's impossible at the moment, the way he's driving into me with fierce determination.

This is about much more than Uther getting off. It's much more than his need to get me out of his system. The way he holds me with steady, gentle hands, the way he buries his face in my hair and inhales. The way his guttural noises are edged with a need beyond sex.

Could he have real feelings? Could this thing between us be real?

Could there be more between us between sweat and spit and cum?

I need more than his body. I need Uther to understand things about me.

As he pounds into me, I tell him the truth.

"I didn't...I didn't come up in society, either. Despite what you assume."

He grunts softly against my throat as he pushes up firmly.

"That's not why I follow you around, Uther. That's not why I look at you the way I do...it has...oh gods...you feel good...it has nothing to do with snobbery."

His voice is a rattle with the effort. Gods, the stamina. "Don't trouble yourself with what I think of you."

"I need you to know...I don't look down on you. I stare because I see ... the most beautiful soul...in your eyes."

Uther pistons his hips harder, but I give back as much as he gives me. "You don't know the first thing...about me..." he rumbles.

But I do. At least, I know all there is to know based on the media reports, the royal watcher blogs, and everything Princess Flora has told me about him.

He's good and pure and built for me. It's as simple as that. Later today, when we've cleaned up and moved on with our daily tasks, my body will remember how perfect this is. I'll be sewing a ballgown for Flora and thinking of him as I sit at my sewing machine. Every press of the pedal will make that soreness radiate through me. I already know this.

"I know you're a good man. I've seen the way you dote on the queen and on the princess. It's enough to make a girl jealous, Uther."

I strangle him with my inner walls, my sweat and my essence combining to drip everywhere, but I don't care.

"You're a fucking trip, little poppy," he says, now thrusting at a furious pace. "...And I love it."

Uther's powerful thrust is so strong that I jerk forward. The large stone over which I am bent jars itself loose and tumbles over the side of the tower.

I scream as I fall forward, but Uther has me. He sets me back on my feet, his arms around my middle.

I watch in horror as the large stone tumbles and shatters on the mossy courtyard below.

"Shit! We broke the castle!" I cry.

Still buried inside me, Uther trembles.

At first, I think he might be crying. "I'm so sorry, Captain. I shouldn't have come." He rests his head against my shoulder and I feel tears soak through my sweater as he bends over me.

Gods almighty, I know the man takes his job seriously, but...

The snort from Uther catches me off guard.

Is he...is he laughing?

"Um, Uther?"

I am jostled as this magnificent man throws his head back in roaring laughter.

In the end, I join his infectious mirth, both of us still in shock and giddy at what's just happened, as if we're two rebellious schoolchildren who've cut class to do vandalism.

When the laughter dies down, I expect him to let me go and send me on my way.

But instead, he holds on to me, hugging me close.

It's not lost on me that he is still buried inside me. I am so full of him that I can hardly keep my knees from buckling.

The cold wind batters my face, blowing my hair back, into his eyes. Chuckling, Uther smoothes my hair down, petting me like a precious pet.

I don't know how long we stay like this, but after some time, the winds begin to ease, and the gray clouds break up.

Uther groans, loud and long. His body stiffens behind me, a massive wall of tense power as he explodes inside me.

His final thrusts are slow and deliberate, his teeth catching the fabric of my sweater at my shoulder, as if to muffle his animalistic sounds. His release comes in long, hot spurts, his body twitching, and yet his gentle hands never let me go. He is always vigilant. Always attentive, and it makes my heart ache.

Uther's spasms finally calm, and I reach back to stroke his freshly shaven cheek.

He gives a full-body sigh, like a prized stallion having a cool-down.

I know we don't have much time, and I know he knows that, too, yet he stays seated inside me, not letting me go.

When I catch my breath, I speak. "I wasn't chosen to be

the palace stylist because of any family connections. My father was a fisherman and my mother worked as a seam-stress. They were killed in the crossfire during the gang wars, and I was taken in by my aunt. She was cruel and I ran away. I raised myself on the streets in the capital."

"Why are you telling me this?" Uther breathes into my sweater, warming my skin.

"Because I'm not what you think I am. And I want you to know me."

In the distance, I hear car wheels on gravel. Someone is coming up the hill.

Once again, Uther's body tenses, and in the next second, he lets me go. I turn around, and he's there, helping me put myself back together, smoothing down my skirt, fixing my sweater, sweeping the dirt off my discarded cape. A wicked half-smirk tugs at his lip as he tends to me.

I must look a wreck. Uther, on the other hand, looks as fresh as he was the moment I spotted him entering the tower. A simple graze of his fingers through his hair, and he looks perfect. It's totally unfair.

"I should let you tend to your queen now," I say, picking up his belt and holster.

His eyes shoot me a warning as he takes his things. "I could have you charged with crimes for touching my weapons."

I roll my eyes, then remember the reason I came here. Well, one of the reasons. "Just one more thing." I reach into my bag to grab my tailor's tape, but Uther stills my hand.

The look in his eye is fierce. "Be in my bed at noon and I'll give you those measurements you want."

"But you said..." He cuts me off with a feral, claiming kiss.

"I said, be in my bed at noon. And don't you fucking shower first."

Dazed, I blink up at him and nod, sighing. "Yes, Captain," I breathe.

I stumble away, half expecting him to slap my ass.

But he doesn't do that. The silent minder would never.

7

ther

I did it.

I got the version of the maddening woman out of my system.

The queen has my undivided attention for the rest of the morning.

There's only one change in plans.

"Your Majesty, might I suggest we move the podium?"

The queen looks at me quizzically, then examining the ruins, notices the freshly destroyed stones that have fallen from the tower and turned to dust at our feet.

"A wise choice," the queen replies, and I order my men to quickly rearrange things, as if the falling stones were a freak accident and not a result of a rousing game of Hide the Bratwurst.

Queen Hilde delivers her speech at Skelside Ruins without any further incident.

The queen's speech is cut short, however, by a sudden rain shower that sends historians and antiquarians ducking for cover. The press retreat to their cars and news vans. The outdoorsy archeologists seem unfazed.

As for me, I'm equally unbothered. I'm always ready for a storm. Don't like the weather in Gravenland? Wait five minutes because another weather system is right behind the one you're in.

Safe under umbrellas, I quickly escort the queen and princess back to their motorcade without a single drop of rain touching their hair nor a speck of mud on their pretty shoes.

I'm feeling proud of myself.

I've rid my mind of that annoying version of the woman that is Sable.

But that doesn't mean I stop thinking about her.

She's been replaced in my mind with what she truly is. A delicate creature who cares deeply and loves hard. A force of nature. A broken child on the inside, the same as me. A person who scrambled her way to the top despite all the barriers set in her way by society. She is softness. She is healing. And she is the most delightfully fierce lover.

The view of the North Sea horizon is replaced by woods and winding paths as the royal motorcade makes its way down the mountain. The woods give way to fields and lakeside cottages, and in the distance is the capital city of Arenhammer with its soaring modern skyscrapers and old-world cathedrals. That is my home. I belong there just as much as anyone else.

It's funny the way a quick rush of chemicals can change

my perspective about myself. At least for the time being. But I know in my heart that what happened between Sable and me was not just a chemical reaction. It was cosmic.

"That went well."

The queen's words snap me out of my reverie.

"Your Majesty? Is there something you need?"

Her gray eyes have something maternal in them when she looks at me.

"No, I need nothing, Uther. Thank you. Just commenting that I feel that event went off well, despite the rain."

The queen is not one to make small talk. It's...unnerving. This sort of chatter always ends up somewhere, and I have to wonder what it is that she wants.

Shit. Perhaps she knows what happened. Maybe she saw Sable and me...is it possible? Am I fired?

A fresh wave of indignation floods me. If Sable is fired, then I'm leaving.

The conclusion I'm jumping to is wild. This is what that woman has done to me. She's not out of my system, she's made me even more mad for her.

And I'm oddly okay with that.

"Your speech was well received, Your Majesty." Giving my opinion feels awkward.

"And what did you think?"

At this, I'm speechless. Even Flora, the princess, who's been furiously texting on her phone, looks up at the queen with an arched eyebrow.

"I...I thought it was interesting and poignant. Educational. I think everyone learned something today."

"And did you? Learn something today?"

In my peripheral vision, I can see Flora's gaze darting between me and the queen.

"I learn something from you every day, Your Majesty. What it takes to be a leader."

To my shock, the queen waves me off with a scoffing laugh. "You can stop kissing my royal ass, Uther."

A snort from Flora threatens to make me break my professional facade.

"I learned that we must treasure our history, no matter how broken and faded it seems."

"Now you're just being poetic. Take the rest of the day off, Uther. You look tired."

What the hell is this?

"Yes, Your Majesty."

"I notice you forgot to give the signal to the drivers. I think you must be overworked."

"Not at all, I'm perfectly—"

She cuts me off. "For the sake of all that's good in the world, I'm cutting back on your hours."

I pause, not quite knowing what she means. "If my services have been inadequate, Your Majesty—"

"Not inadequate in the least," the queen interrupts. "But with the way this family is headed, if there's one thing I learned from raising my children, it's that I've placed too many expectations on them. And we have been asking too much of our staff. Let's face it, this monarchy isn't making laws of any significance. It's time to scale back."

Quickly, I mentally search through my contacts to determine if there's a second job I can procure. The queen picks up on my moment of panic. "Oh, don't worry. We're keeping you on. I'll pay you full-time wages if you agree to stay, but also agree to work less."

Perhaps since the king passed away, the queen is realizing she can't operate at the same clip as she always has. Or maybe she regrets controlling every aspect of her children's lives, and the fact that several of them no longer speak to her. Whatever it is, the queen is changing before my very eyes.

"Very well, I agree to your terms."

She rubs her palms together as if washing off the day's hard work. "Excellent. That's sorted. Perhaps now that stylist of yours can finally lasso you with that tape she carries around her neck. Gods know you're a difficult one to pin down."

The queen doesn't meet my gaze. She's done with this conversation and instead turns her attention to the quickly approaching city skyline.

Flora's shocked eyes catch mine. I struggle to maintain my unflappable presence. The princess bites her lip and returns to whomever she's texting, tapping away furiously on her screen.

The long and short of it is this: I'll have more free time.

More time for myself. More time for Sable. More chances to explore every whim with her. More opportunities to have my way with her, to fill her with my seed, to see her belly rounded with our children.

And I'll be staying employed by the palace indefinitely, which means I'll be able to provide for our children, and even our children's children.

The queen practically decreed it. We have to do this now, I think wryly.

I know what people say about me. The silent minder takes his job far too seriously. Gravenlanders are a relaxed, fun-loving people. The most I ever have to worry about is the occasional drunk reveler getting too close to the queen. Or a tiresome diplomat taking up too much of her time. I approach every moment of every day as if the queen and the princess's life depends on my vigilance.

Better to be too careful than to let my guard down and risk the lives of my staff.

Still, what can I do if the queen wishes me to work less?

The queen practically decreed that Sable and I end up together, so what other choice do we have?

8

S able

"I thought I told you not to bathe."

I know Uther's words came out rougher than intended. Fortunately, I am who I am, and I take this in stride.

I am in Uther's chamber, where he ordered me to be. I waited for hours, so yes, I did bathe. And now, I'm perched on the edge of his deep-soak tub in his private quarters in the palace.

I answer with a teasing smile. "I didn't think you were serious about that," I say.

Cranking off the running water that fills the tub with steaming, rose-scented bubbles, I look up to find a completely naked Uther standing in the doorway.

My breath catches in my throat. I'm not prepared for all of this. The barrel chest, tattooed arms, soft swirls of hair across his pecs. So much to stare at. So much to enjoy. Just... so much.

Uther's cock, dark pink and veiny, stands at full mast as he watches me.

My mouth salivates.

"I should put you over my knee. I meant it when I said I could have you in front of a judge by lunchtime."

My half-smile expands to a full megawatt grin. "Or you could say, 'Thank you, Sable, for drawing me a bath.'"

His gaze darts downward to the split in my satiny robe.

He says nothing further but approaches me with a slow swagger, a wicked glint in his eyes. My nipples tighten.

Am I going to let him reach down and untie my robe? Apparently so.

Will I just sit here and let him push my robe open, let his eyes worship my breasts like he owns me?

Yes. Looks like I'll be doing that, too.

The robe falls away, held up around my waist by the small ties there. I must look ridiculous, but I don't have time to think about that as Uther takes what's his. His rough hands warm my breasts as he takes two overflowing handfuls. I swallow hard, willing myself not to grab him and plunge his face between my legs once again.

He kneels in front of me, massaging my breasts, sweeping his calloused thumbs over my sensitive nipples. I bite down on my lip.

"Thank you, little poppy."

The nickname sparks a primal desire that begins behind my navel. It builds when he lowers his head and takes one nipple into that wicked mouth. And when he sucks in long, decadent pulls, I feel as if I might slide off the edge of the tub.

I nearly come apart when he scrapes his teeth over that

sensitive bud. This is so much. So fast. As much as I love it, there are things to be discussed.

"Uther," I breathe.

He pops one nipple out of his mouth and ravishes the opposite one. So slowly. So the opposite of the hurried rutting we did earlier today.

The man takes his time, worshiping my body. So much time that I'm trembling with need in his arms. I thread my fingers through his damp locks.

"Look at you," he croons. "All for me."

"Wouldn't it be a shame to waste these bubbles?"

I've unlocked something in the silent minder. Something deep and wild and unhinged. With a look of pure mischief, Uther steps over me and sinks down into the tub. I smile at the picture of this brutish-looking man covered in pink bubbles. Before I can comprehend what's happening, Uther reaches forward and tugs loose the ties at my waist. My satin robe cascades to the floor, but I don't protest.

Neither do I complain when he lifts me into the tub as if I weigh nothing, sending waves of hot water and sprays of pink bubbles flying over the rim onto the slate floor.

He holds me against his chest, warm and wet.

"Smells like you," he says.

I smile against the soft fur and run my thumb over his nipple. "It's my signature perfume-scented bubble bath. Sorry if it smells girly, I couldn't find anything in your room that was suitable."

"It smells like you. If anyone has a problem with me smelling like you, I don't care."

I can't help the grin on my face as he cuddles me against him. "I like you."

"You'd better. We're going to be spending a hell of a lot more time together."

Lifting my head to meet his gaze, I ask. "You mean while I make your new uniforms?"

He smiles. "No. I mean you and me. Us. Spending time together."

For a moment, I panic. "Oh, no. Did I get you fired?" But wait, that's ridiculous. If he were fired, we wouldn't be here, in his personal chambers. He'd be packing, wouldn't he? "Or...demoted?"

Chuckling, he says, "No, love. We're going to be spending more time together because the queen fucking decreed it."

My eyes blink in confusion. "Decreed it?"

"That's what I said. Which means we can never break up. It's the law now."

I study his face to determine if he's joking, but there's no sign of that.

"Well, if it's the law," I croon.

"Under penalty of banishment from the kingdom," he says. "I'm yours."

Mine. The silent minder, the chief of the security, the most eligible bachelor in the palace, is no longer eligible. He is mine, and I am his. Mystifyingly, because the queen said so?

Whatever. I'll take it and run with it. That's what I do.

And then I take Uther's hard length in hand. His low groan fills me with a deeper satisfaction than I've ever thought possible...he fills me with promises, and with joy, and with unlimited possibilities.

That doesn't change the fact that I still have work to do.

But that can wait.

We have our whole lives ahead of us.

• • •

THE END

Thank you for reading Reckless in Ruins! If you enjoyed this book, please consider leaving a review on Amazon.

For more high-heat, obsessed bodyguard vibes, check out:

The Bodyguard and His Bunny

or

Officer Max

WHERE IT ALL BEGAN...

Turn the page to read the first chapter from Favored Prince —book one in the Reckless Royals series!

FAVORED PRINCE

CHAPTER ONE

Torben

The stone bell tower chimes midnight over the packed plaza, prompting the festive crowd's eruption with cheers, noisemakers and air horns.

"Aren't you special?" The gruff voice next to me in the balcony box drips with irony. Sigurd knows how much I detest this particular tradition.

I turn to my right and beam at my brother with a practiced smile that delivers a sneer only a brother can see. "Jealous?"

Sigurd's unmanaged beard twitches. "Jealous of the heir apparent? Brother, I'm grateful to still be a bachelor with no expectations from anybody."

The person to my left finally speaks, slurring his words. "Except psychopathy."

Here we go.

The flash in Sigurd's eyes serves as the first warning.

Wanting to defuse this exchange before it becomes a situation, I lean to the left and place a brotherly hand on the shoulder of the slightly teetering Etienne, attempting to force his glassy eyes to focus on me and not on our youngest brother.

"Not here. Not now," I urge Etienne. Our mother, the queen, gives us a subtle side-eye while waving at the cheering crowd.

Etienne, undeterred, leans backward to address Sigurd with a wagging forefinger. "The first sign of a psychopath is poor treatment of animals."

The thickly-bearded one simmers next to me. "Where do you think your hangover duck sandwiches come from? Hunters, you imbecile."

Etienne laughs, "Your friend, the gamekeeper, rounds them up for you. Not much of a fair fight if you ask me."

At the mention of the gamekeeper, our baby sister, Princess Flora, looks up from her knitting. She wants to say something, but then changes her mind and returns to her project.

On the twelfth bell, the queen leans behind Etienne and hisses to me, "Order."

The crowd bursts into "Happy Birthday, Prince Torben."

I can't bear listening to this, but I'm happy for a distraction. Our mother has cued me to get control of everyone now, or I'll hear about it later.

I subtly nudge Etienne. "Stop goading Sig. For my sake."

"It's too easy," Etienne chuckles.

At my right, Sig is still eyeing our drunken brother, barely pretending to maintain a serene face for the public.

"Smile," I remind him. "The paps are watching."

"Good; I hope they catch the royal introduction of my fist to Etienne's groceries."

"For me. Ignore the little bastard, just this once. You owe me."

Sig stiffens, and that god-awful beard twitches again. He knows what for. He harrumphs but otherwise tries to ignore the other brother.

The crowd below transitions into the Gravenland national anthem. Oh god. This will take a while.

I lean behind Sig and gesture to Flora.

She looks up from her sweater project—I swear I don't know who she's knitting sweaters for when her wardrobe is choked with finery sent from designers the world over—and frowns.

"What are you waving those pretty gloved hands at me for, brother? I'm minding my business," she says.

"Stand up," I tell her in my most stern big brother voice.

"Why?"

"Because everyone can see you!"

"I'm trying to work this knot out."

"Flora, please."

"I'm not bothering anybody, and this song will last an hour. You can't expect me to stand through the entire thing."

This. This is why I don't like to be put in charge of my siblings. I am not their parent. But I've more or less been forced into that role from the time we were all children.

And now, I'm 35, and it appears the only way out of this parental role is to get married, move out of the palace, and begin bossing around a family of my own. Oh, joy.

"Flora," I growl through gritted teeth.

With a dirty glare and a hissed, "Why don't you get laid already and leave the rest of us alone," Flora stands but refuses to set down her handmade wooden needles, a precious gift sent to her by an adoring fan. It's sweet that she's taken such a liking to such a simple present. I give most everything away to charity, whatever they will accept. Not because I'm such a goody-goody, but I don't like to be reminded that I have *fans.*

Not that I've earned admirers. I was born in the public eye, and I'm doomed to remain there.

I lack Flora's sentimentality, and it's one of the things I admire in my sister.

She waves at the crowd, joining in on the third verse of the Gravenland national anthem.

The cameras will only show the happy, smiling faces of the six members of the royal family, all basking in the good wishes of their citizens.

What they don't see is Flora quietly in a snit. Sig barely controlling his temper. Me, exhausted and searching for new excuses about why I'm not interested in this or that nobleman's daughter on this, my 35th birthday. Etienne, halfway to being drunk off his ass and smirking. The queen, having had it with all of us. And the king, down at the other end of the balcony box? The king is happily oblivious to all of us.

Because he is bound and determined to marry me off, once and for all.

By the time the crowd below us has gotten around to the fifth verse of the world's longest national anthem, something snaps on either side of me. Etienne makes a big show of joining the crowd in song, lifting his goblet above his head merrily and pumping his fist. The crowd goes nuts at his antics, not knowing he's mocking the entire thing. In his state of compromised judgment, he looks past me and thrusts his goblet on the long high note. Wine splashes out, spilling deep red drops all over Sig's face and beard.

Sig loses it. He hurls himself over me in one rather

impressive leap, grabbing Etienne by his overcoat lapels. The impact knocks the golden goblet out of Etienne's hand. I lunge for it as it tumbles over the balcony's edge. But it's too late. I watch in horror as the bejeweled vessel falls to the ground below, spilling wine all over the fascinator hat of a visiting dignitary.

Haplessly, Etienne stretches his arm over the railing toward the goblet. Sig's face gets in the way of Etienne's reach. In seconds, it's a fully involved fistfight.

Where are the security guards? Probably rushing to the aid of the poor woman with the wine-soaked fascinator.

Not that they'd be any help up here; they usually let me break up the fights between siblings because they're all too scared to lay hands on the royal family.

In my attempt to separate the two brothers, I tug too hard, and Etienne stumbles backward, then overcompensates and stumbles forward again drunkenly, dangerously close to tumbling over the edge.

Grabbing a fistful of his cloak, I wrench the fool back from the edge, sending him tumbling to the floor of the balcony box.

And in my attempt to hold the drunkard back from the edge, I fail to notice what is happening to my right.

A feminine shriek makes my blood run cold while Etienne looks past me in horror.

The final note of the Gravenland national anthem is quickly drowned out by astonished shouts as the crowd nearest us catches on to what's happening.

I whip around. My brain registers that Flora no longer stands where she'd been, but it doesn't connect that fact with why Sig leans dangerously over the balcony's edge.

The queen lets out a bloodcurdling scream. The king

bellows angrily, like he's being merely inconvenienced, "What is it now?"

I rush to the ledge, only to see Flora hanging on by a thread.

Literally.

One of Flora's hands clutches a thick wooden needle, around which a loop of yarn is cinched in a jumbled knot. At the other end of that thread is our brother, Sig, holding on for dear life. I scan the horrifying tableau, and my stomach threatens to send my dinner back up. At my feet, the half-finished sweater sits in a pile.

The yarn pulls so tightly I can see it cutting into Sig's hand. Calloused though they may be from a lifetime of climbing rocks and wrestling bears or whatever the hell he gets up to, he grimaces in pain.

Someone's shoulder joint gives a sickening pop. Adrenaline courses through me, and the next thing I know, I've got both hands in front of Sig's, but it's not enough of a hold to do any good.

I can pull Flora up if I reach more of the yarn and persuade Sig to let go. He may be bigger than me, but I'm twice the weight of our baby sister.

"Let go, Sig. I've got her."

With a curse, Sig tells me to shut up, and tugs with his good arm. The yarn is so taut it's cutting into his flesh to the point of bleeding. I'm not a soft one by any means, but no one has more callouses than Sig.

"Etienne!" I cry out. "We need you!"

"I can help!" Etienne shouts with uncharacteristic, unbridled excitement.

I don't dare take my eyes off my sister, who's looking up at me, her big brother, to save the day.

"I've got hold of the yarn! Let go before you dislocate

your other shoulder, Sig, you idiot." Etienne sounds author-
itative for the first time in his life, and I feel a flash of pride.

Neither of us looks at Etienne, but Sig snarls in pain as
the wool slips through his other hand. "I can't hold it!"

Sig refuses to let go, but Etienne is shouting. "I'm
anchoring it! I've got it; you can let go."

Meanwhile, security and hotel employees are scrambling, five stories below us, on the plaza, to clear the area to
make way for a rescue squad. Revelers are instead insisting
that they can catch Flora if she lets go. But we all know that
won't end well for anyone.

"Don't make me regret this, Etienne!" Sig releases the
yarn, and we turn to look at our brother. Etienne holds the
unfinished sweater and his grip, looking proud of himself.

A fresh wave of panic surges through me in that instant
when we all realize—too late—that the yarn is unraveling
itself row by row by row by horrifying row at an alarming
speed.

I don't hesitate. I run inside the building, shoving past
the guards, bounding down five flights of stairs. I burst
through the hotel doors and prepare myself for the worst
moment of my life.

But the worst moment never comes.

Someone has caught Flora.

Setting aside my shock and disbelief, I close the
distance between myself and the unknown citizen holding
my sister, intending to thank him profusely. This is like
trying to run headlong into a maze, until people realize
who I am.

The crowd parts like the Red Sea, and there before me is
Flora. Alone, clutching one needle.

I catch up to her and shield her from the gawkers. Her
frame trembles in my arms.

"Brother, I'm okay." Her eyes are wide and look right through me. She's in shock, not wholly aware of herself.

"Who caught you?"

Flora's face is ghost white as she shakes her head. "He's gone."

I glimpse a tall, dark-haired fellow ducking his way through the crowd, away from us.

I try to bring her back to earth with a joke. "Thank God someone made those needles for you. They should be commended."

She shakes her head again.

"How did that man catch me?"

My sister is shaking like a leaf, so there's only one thing to do. I scoop her up and begin calling out for a medic.

END OF PREVIEW

MORE BY ABBY KNOX

All Abby's books are stand-alone romances, each with its own HEA. No cliffhangers or cheating!

Abby's latest releases:

Fix Me Up (single dad)

Followed by the CEO (insta obsession, 'light' stalking)

Filthy Chef (workplace romance/one-night-stand-turned HEA)

Reckless Royals

Favored Prince (royal family/American bride)

Bad Prince (forced marriage/divorce pact)

Wild Prince (Forced proximity)

Forgotten Prince (mariage pact)

Stolen Crown (brother's best friend)

Related short story: Reckless in Ruins

Roadside Attractions series:

Roadside Attraction (insta love)

Claiming Fate (rivals to lovers)

Falling into Fate (long lost friends to lovers)

Fate's Dark Shadows (age gap)

Rode Hard (insta love, dating app)

Crash into Me (grumpy mountain man)

Snowed Under (second chance, later-in-life)

Wish List (holiday, older heroine/younger hero)

Fate's Holi-Date (he falls first, age gap)

Wood Brothers series

(OTT alpha insta-love. Set in same world as Roadside Attractions.)

Nailed

Screwed

Drilled

Love Games series

(OTT insta love, nerdy-but-hot heroes. Set in same world as Roadside Attractions.)

Roll For Initiative

Roll for Damage

Roll for Charisma

The Mail-Order Brides of Darling Creek

(tropes include: age gap, mail/e-mail order brides, small town, insta love, cowboy)

A Baby for the Bride

A Week to Wed

Her Guardian Groom

The Cowboy Auction of Darling Creek

(tropes include: dating auction, small town, cowboy, insta love)

The Cowgirl's Bid

Winning the Cowboy

Her Forbidden Prize

Small-Town Gossip

(Set in Darling Creek, Montana. Tropes include: small town, insta love, workplace romance)

Do That To Me

Say That To Me

Love That For Me

Paradise Passions

(vacation romances)

Babymoon

Honeymoon Hideout

Need more stand alones?

Are You For Reel?

The Bodyguard and His Bunny

A Little Amusement

511 Kissme Lane

V-Card Vacation

Hail Mary

Holiday short reads

Elf-napped

Bagged by the Elf

Wish List

Snow-plowed

The Christmas Pickup

The Halloween Bet

The Halloween Flip

Pumpkin King

Snow-plowed

Additional titles are available on iBooks, Barnes & Noble, Everand, Smashwords, Fable, and more.

For signed paperbacks, exclusive downloads, and more, visit Abby's website at authorabbyknox.com

Happy reading!

ABOUT THE AUTHOR

Abby Knox writes feel-good, high-heat romance that readers have described as quirky, sexy, adorable, and hilarious. Her favorite tropes include: Forced proximity, opposites attract, grumpy/sunshine, age gap, boss/employee, fated mates/insta-love, and more. She is heavily influenced by Buffy the Vampire Slayer, Gilmore Girls, and LOST. But don't worry, she won't ever make you suffer like Luke & Lorelai. Abby lives in North Caroline with her family.

Say hello at authorabbyknox@gmail.com

Find links to all of Abby's social media pages at
authorabbyknox.com

Milton Keynes UK
Ingram Content Group UK Ltd.
UKHW021134080824
446563UK00015B/588

9 798227 094872